CHRISTMAS
WITH DULL
PEOPLE

D1494031

CHRISTMAS WITH DULL PEOPLE

SAKI

Daunt Books

This edition first published in
Great Britain in 2017 by
Daunt Books
83 Marylebone High Street
London W1U 4QW

1

A CIP catalogue record for this title is
available from the British Library.

ISBN 978-1-911547-18-1

Typeset by Marsha Swan

Printed and bound by TJ International

www.dauntbookspublishing.co.uk

Contents

CHRISTMAS
WITH DULL
PEOPLE

REGINALD'S
CHRISTMAS
REVEL

*T*hey say (said Reginald) that there's nothing sadder than victory except defeat. If you've ever stayed with dull people during what is alleged to be the festive season, you can probably revise that saying. I shall never forget putting in a Christmas at the Babwolds'. Mrs Babwold is some relation of my father's — a sort of to-be-left-till-called-for cousin — and that was considered sufficient reason for my having to accept her invitation at about the sixth time of asking; though why the sins of the father should be visited by the children — you won't find any notepaper in that drawer; that's where I keep old menus and first-night programmes.

Mrs Babwold wears a rather solemn personality, and has never been known to smile, even when saying disagreeable things to her friends or making out the Stores list. She takes her pleasures sadly. A state elephant at a durbar gives one a very similar impression. Her husband gardens in all weathers. When a man goes out in the pouring rain to brush caterpillars off rose trees, I generally imagine his life indoors leaves something to be desired; anyway, it must be very unsettling for the caterpillars.

Of course there were other people there. There was a Major Somebody who had shot things in Lapland, or somewhere of that sort; I forget what they were, but it wasn't for want of reminding. We had them cold with every meal almost, and he was continually giving us details of what they measured from tip to tip, as though he thought we were going to make them warm underthings for the winter. I used to listen to him with a rapt attention that I thought rather suited me, and then one day I quite modestly gave the dimensions of an okapi I had shot in the Lincolnshire fens. The Major turned a beautiful Tyrian scarlet (I remember thinking at the time that I should like my bathroom hung in that colour), and I think that at that moment he almost found it in his heart to dislike me. Mrs Babwold put on a first-aid-to-the-injured expression, and asked him why he didn't publish a book of his sporting reminiscences; it would be SO interesting. She didn't remember till afterwards that he had given her two fat volumes on the subject, with his portrait and autograph as a frontispiece and an appendix on the habits of the Arctic mussel.

It was in the evening that we cast aside the cares and distractions of the day and really lived. Cards were thought to be too frivolous and empty a way of passing the time, so most of them played what they called a book game. You went out into the hall – to get an inspiration, I suppose – then you came in again with a muffler tied round your neck and looked silly, and the others were supposed to guess that you were *Wee MacGreegor*. I held out against the inanity as long as I decently could, but at last, in a lapse of good nature, I consented to masquerade as a book, only I warned them that it would take some time to carry out. They waited for the best part of forty minutes, while I went and played wineglass skittles with the pageboy in the pantry; you play it with a champagne cork, you know, and the one who knocks down the most glasses without breaking them wins. I won, with four unbroken out of seven; I think William suffered from over-anxiousness. They were rather mad in the drawing room at my not having come back, and they weren't a bit pacified when I told them afterwards that I was *At the End of the Passage*.

'I never did like Kipling,' was Mrs Babwold's comment, when the situation dawned upon her. 'I couldn't see anything clever in *Earthworms out of Tuscany* – or is that by Darwin?'

Of course these games are very educational, but, personally, I prefer bridge.

On Christmas evening we were supposed to be specially festive in the Old English fashion. The hall was horribly draughty, but it seemed to be the proper place to revel in, and it was decorated with Japanese fans and Chinese lanterns, which gave it a very Old English effect. A young lady with a confidential voice favoured us with a long recitation about a little girl who died or did something equally hackneyed, and then the Major gave us a graphic account of a struggle he had with a wounded bear. I privately wished that the bears would win sometimes on these occasions; at least they wouldn't go vapouring about it afterwards. Before we had time to recover our spirits, we were indulged with some thought-reading by a young man whom one knew instinctively had a good mother and an indifferent tailor – the sort of young man who talks unflaggingly through the thickest soup, and smooths his hair dubiously as though he thought it might hit back. The thought-reading was rather a success; he announced that the hostess was thinking about poetry, and she admitted that her mind was dwelling on one of Austin's odes. Which was near enough. I fancy she had been really wondering whether a scrag end of mutton and some cold plum pudding would do for the kitchen dinner next day. As a crowning dissipation, they all sat down to play progressive halma, with milk chocolate for prizes. I've been carefully brought up, and I don't like to play games of skill for milk chocolate, so I invented a headache and retired from the scene. I had been preceded a few minutes earlier by Miss Langshan-Smith, a rather formidable lady, who always got up at some uncomfortable hour in the morning, and gave you the impression that

D
B

Daunt Books Publishing

Founded in 2010, the
Daunt Books imprint is
dedicated to publishing
brilliant works by talented
authors from around the world.
Our titles are inspired
by the Daunt Books shops
themselves, and the exciting
atmosphere of discovery to be
found in a good bookshop.

www.dauntbooks.co.uk

publishing@dauntbooks.co.uk

Our Authors

Saki

Sybille Bedford

Jiří Weil

Mark Twain

C S Godshalk

Ann Bridge

Paul Watkins

Stefan Heym

O Henry

K J Orr

Christa Wolf

Simon Loftus

G B Stern

Virginia Woolf

Philip Langeskov

Nathanael West

Mahesh Rao

James Buchan

Sarah Pickstone

Madeleine Bourdouxhe

S N Behrman

Julianne Pachico

Machado de Assis

Laura van den Berg

Bapsi Sidhwa

Leonard Michaels

John McPhee

Vivian Gornick

Lawrence Sutin

she had been in communication with most of the European Governments before breakfast. There was a paper pinned on her door with a signed request that she might be called particularly early on the morrow. Such an opportunity does not come twice in a lifetime. I covered up everything except the signature with another notice, to the effect that before these words should meet the eye she would have ended a misspent life, was sorry for the trouble she was giving, and would like a military funeral. A few minutes later I violently exploded an air-filled paper bag on the landing, and gave a stage moan that could have been heard in the cellars. Then I pursued my original intention and went to bed. The noise those people made in forcing open the good lady's door was positively indecorous; she resisted gallantly, but I believe they searched her for bullets for about a quarter of an hour, as if she had been an historic battlefield.

I hate travelling on Boxing Day, but one must occasionally do things that one dislikes.

REGINALD ON CHRISTMAS PRESENTS

I wish it to be distinctly understood (said Reginald) that I don't want a George, Prince of Wales Prayer Book as a Christmas present. The fact cannot be too widely known.

There ought (he continued) to be technical education classes on the science of present-giving. No one seems to have the faintest notion of what anyone else wants, and the prevalent ideas on the subject are not creditable to a civilised community.

There is, for instance, the female relative in the country who 'knows a tie is always useful', and sends you some spotted horror that you could only wear in secret or in Tottenham Court Road. It might have been useful had she kept it to tie up currant bushes with, when it would have served the double purpose of supporting the branches and frightening away the birds — for it is an admitted fact that the ordinary tomtit of commerce has a sounder aesthetic taste than the average female relative in the country.

Then there are aunts. They are always a difficult class to deal with in the matter of presents. The trouble is that one never catches them really young enough. By the time one has educated them to an appreciation of the fact that one does not wear red woollen mittens in the West End, they die, or quarrel with the family, or do something equally inconsiderate. That is why the supply of trained aunts is always so precarious.

There is my Aunt Agatha, *par exemple*, who sent me a pair of gloves last Christmas, and even got so far as to choose a kind that was being worn and had the correct number of buttons. But — they were nines! I sent them to a boy whom I hated intimately: he didn't wear them, of course, but he could have — that was where the bitterness of death came in. It was nearly as consoling as sending white flowers to his funeral. Of course I wrote and told my aunt that they were the one thing that had been wanting to make existence blossom like a rose; I am afraid she thought me frivolous — she comes from the North, where they live in the fear of Heaven and the Earl of Durham. (Reginald affects an exhaustive knowledge of things political, which furnishes an excellent excuse for not discussing them.) Aunts with a dash of foreign extraction in them are the most satisfactory in the way of understanding these things; but if you can't choose your aunt, it is wisest in the long run to choose the present and send her the bill.

Even friends of one's own set, who might be expected to know better, have curious delusions on the subject. I am not collecting copies of the cheaper editions of Omar Khayyam. I gave the last four that I received to the liftboy, and I like to think of him reading them, with FitzGerald's notes, to his aged mother. Liftboys always have aged mothers; shows such nice feeling on their part, I think.

Personally, I can't see where the difficulty in choosing suitable presents lies. No boy who had brought himself up properly could fail to appreciate one of those decorative bottles of liqueurs that are so reverently staged in Morel's window – and it wouldn't in the least matter if one did get duplicates. And there would always be the supreme moment of dreadful uncertainty whether it was crème de menthe or chartreuse – like the expectant thrill on seeing your partner's hand turned up at bridge. People may say what they like about the decay of Christianity; the religious system that produced green chartreuse can never really die.

And then, of course, there are liqueur glasses, and crystallised fruits, and tapestry curtains, and heaps of other necessaries of life that make really sensible presents – not to speak of luxuries, such as having one's bills paid, or getting something quite sweet in the way of jewellery. Unlike the alleged Good Woman of the Bible, I'm not above rubies. When found, by the way, she must have been rather a problem at Christmas-time; nothing short of a blank cheque would have fitted the situation. Perhaps it's as well that she's died out.

The great charm about me (concluded Reginald) is that I am so easily pleased.

But I draw the line at a Prince of Wales Prayer Book.

BERTIE'S
CHRISTMAS
EVE

*I*t was Christmas Eve, and the family circle of Luke Steffink, Esq., was aglow with the amiability and random mirth which the occasion demanded. A long and lavish dinner had been partaken of, waits had been round and sung carols; the house party had regaled itself with more carolling on its own account, and there had been romping which, even in a pulpit reference, could not have been condemned as ragging. In the midst of the general glow, however, there was one black unkindled cinder.

Bertie Steffink, nephew of the aforementioned Luke, had early in life adopted the profession of ne'er-do-well; his father had been something of the kind before him. At the age of eighteen Bertie had commenced that round of visits to our colonial possessions, so seemly and desirable in the case of a Prince of the Blood, so suggestive of insincerity in a young man of the middle-class. He had gone to grow tea in Ceylon and fruit in British Columbia, and to help sheep to grow wool in Australia. At the age of twenty he had just returned from some similar errand in Canada, from which it may be gathered that the trial he gave to these various experiments was of the summary drum-head nature. Luke Steffink, who fulfilled the troubled role of guardian and deputy-parent to Bertie, deplored the persistent manifestation of the homing instinct on his nephew's part, and his solemn thanks earlier in the day for the blessing of reporting a united family had no reference to Bertie's return.

Arrangements had been promptly made for packing the youth off to a distant corner of Rhodesia, whence return would be a difficult matter; the journey to this uninviting destination was imminent, in fact a more careful and willing traveller would have already begun to think about his packing. Hence Bertie was in no mood to share in the festive spirit which displayed itself around him, and resentment smouldered within him at the eager, self-absorbed discussion of social plans for the coming months which he heard on all sides. Beyond depressing his uncle and the family circle generally by singing 'Say au revoir, and not goodbye', he had taken no part in the evening's conviviality.

Eleven o'clock had struck some half-hour ago, and the elder Steffinks began to throw out suggestions leading up to that process which they called retiring for the night.

'Come, Teddie, it's time you were in your little bed, you know,' said Luke Steffink to his thirteen-year-old son.

'That's where we all ought to be,' said Mrs Steffink.

'There wouldn't be room,' said Bertie.

The remark was considered to border on the scandalous; everybody ate raisins and almonds with the nervous industry of sheep feeding during threatening weather.

'In Russia,' said Horace Bordenby, who was staying in the house as a Christmas guest, 'I've read that the peasants believe that if you go into a cow-house or stable at midnight on Christmas Eve you will hear the animals talk. They're supposed to have the gift of speech at that one moment of the year.'

'Oh, DO let's ALL go down to the cow-house and listen to what they've got to say!' exclaimed Beryl, to whom anything was thrilling and amusing if you did it in a troop.

Mrs Steffink made a laughing protest, but gave a virtual consent by saying, 'We must all wrap up well, then.' The idea seemed a scatter-brained one to her, and almost heathenish, but it afforded an opportunity for 'throwing the young people together', and as such she welcomed it. Mr Horace Bordenby was a young man with quite substantial prospects, and he had danced with Beryl at a local subscription ball a sufficient number of times to warrant the authorised enquiry on the part of the neighbours whether 'there was anything in it'. Though Mrs Steffink would not have put it in so many words, she shared the idea of the Russian peasantry that on this night the beast might speak.

The cow-house stood at the junction of the garden with a small paddock, an isolated survival, in a suburban neighbourhood, of what had once been a small farm. Luke Steffink was complacently proud of his cow-house and his two cows; he felt that they gave him a stamp of solidity which no number of Wyandottes or Orpingtons could impart. They even seemed to link him in a sort of inconsequent way with those patriarchs who derived importance from their floating capital of flocks and herbs, he-asses and she-asses. It had been an anxious and momentous occasion when he had had to decide definitely between 'the Byre' and 'the Ranch' for the naming of his villa residence. A December midnight was hardly the moment he would have chosen for showing his farm building to visitors, but since it was a fine night, and the young people were anxious for an excuse for a mild frolic, Luke consented to chaperon the expedition. The servants had long since gone to bed, so the house was left in charge of Bertie, who scornfully declined to stir out on the pretext of listening to bovine conversation.

'We must go quietly,' said Luke, as he headed the procession of giggling young folk, brought up in the rear by the shawled and hooded figure of Mrs Steffink; 'I've always laid stress on keeping this a quiet and orderly neighbourhood.'

It was a few minutes to midnight when the party reached the cow-house and made its way in by the light of Luke's stable lantern. For a moment everyone stood in silence, almost with a feeling of being in church.

'Daisy – the one lying down – is by a short-horn bull out of a Guernsey cow,' announced Luke in a hushed voice, which was in keeping with the foregoing impression.

'Is she?' said Bordenby, rather as if he had expected her to be by Rembrandt.

'Myrtle is—'

Myrtle's family history was cut short by a little scream from the women of the party.

The cow-house door had closed noiselessly behind them and the key had turned gratingly in the lock; then they heard Bertie's voice pleasantly wishing them goodnight and his footsteps retreating along the garden path.

Luke Steffink strode to the window; it was a small square opening of the old-fashioned sort, with iron bars let into the stonework.

'Unlock the door this instant,' he shouted, with as much air of menacing authority as a

29

hen might assume when screaming through the bars of a coop at a marauding hawk. In reply to his summons the hall door closed with a defiant bang.

A neighbouring clock struck the hour of midnight. If the cows had received the gift of human speech at that moment they would not have been able to make themselves heard. Seven or eight other voices were engaged in describing Bertie's present conduct and his general character at a high pressure of excitement and indignation.

In the course of half an hour or so everything that it was permissible to say about Bertie had been said some dozens of times, and other topics began to come to the front – the extreme mustiness of the cow-house, the possibility of it catching fire and the probability of it being a Rowton House for the vagrant rats of the neighbourhood. And still no sign of deliverance came to the unwilling vigil-keepers.

Towards one o'clock the sound of rather

boisterous and undisciplined carol singing approached rapidly, and came to a sudden anchorage, apparently just outside the garden gate. A motor-load of youthful 'bloods', in a high state of conviviality, had made a tempo- rary halt for repairs; the stoppage, however, did not extend to the vocal efforts of the party, and the watchers in the cow-shed were treated to a highly unauthorised rendering of 'Good King Wenceslas', in which the adjective 'good' appeared to be very carelessly applied.

The noise had the effect of bringing Bertie out into the garden, but he utterly ignored the pale, angry faces peering out at the cow-house window, and concentrated his attention on the revellers outside the gate.

'Wassail, you chaps!' he shouted.

'Wassail, old sport!' they shouted back; 'we'd jolly well drink y'r health, only we've nothing to drink it in.'

'Come and wassail inside,' said Bertie hospi- tably; 'I'm all alone, and there's heaps of "wet".'

They were total strangers, but his touch of kindness made them instantly his kin. In another moment the unauthorised version of King Wenceslas, which, like many other scandals, grew worse on repetition, went echoing up the garden path; two of the revellers gave an impromptu performance on the way by executing the stair-case waltz up the terraces of what Luke Steffink, hitherto with some justification, called his rock garden. The rock part of it was still there when the waltz had been accorded its third encore. Luke, more than ever like a cooped hen behind the cow-house bars, was in a position to realise the feelings of concert-goers unable to counter-mand the call for an encore which they neither desire or deserve.

The hall door closed with a bang on Bertie's guests, and the sounds of merriment became faint and muffled to the weary watchers at the other end of the garden. Presently two ominous pops, in quick succession, made themselves distinctly heard.

'They've got at the champagne!' exclaimed Mrs Steffink.

'Perhaps it's the sparkling Moselle,' said Luke hopefully.

Three or four more pops were heard.

'The champagne and the sparkling Moselle,' said Mrs Steffink.

Luke uncorked an expletive which, like brandy in a temperance household, was only used on rare emergencies. Mr Horace Bordenby had been making use of similar expressions under his breath for a considerable time past. The experiment of 'throwing the young people together' had been prolonged beyond a point when it was likely to produce any romantic result.

Some forty minutes later the hall door opened and disgorged a crowd that had thrown off any restraint of shyness that might have influenced its earlier actions. Its vocal efforts in the direction of carol singing were now supplemented by instrumental music; a Christmas tree that had been prepared for the children of the gardener and other household retainers had yielded a rich spoil of tin trumpets, rattles and drums. The life story of King Wenceslas had been dropped, Luke was thankful to notice, but it was intensely irritating for the chilled prisoners in the cow-house to be told that it was a hot time in the old town tonight, together with some accurate but entirely superfluous information as to the imminence of Christmas morning. Judging by the protests which began to be shouted from the upper windows of neighbouring houses the sentiments prevailing in the cow-house were heartily echoed in other quarters.

The revellers found their car, and, what was more remarkable, managed to drive off in it, with a parting fanfare of tin trumpets. The lively beat of a drum disclosed the fact that the master of the revels remained on the scene.

'Bertie!' came in an angry, imploring chorus of shouts and screams from the cow-house window.

'Hullo,' cried the owner of the name, turning his rather errant steps in the direction of the summons; 'are you people still there? Must have heard everything cows got to say by this time. If you haven't, no use waiting. After all, it's a Russian legend, and Russian Chrismush Eve not due for 'nother fortnight. Better come out.'

After one or two ineffectual attempts he managed to pitch the key of the cow-house door in through the window. Then, lifting his voice in the strains of 'I'm afraid to go home in the dark', with a lusty drum accompaniment, he led the way back to the house. The hurried procession of the released that followed in his steps came in for a good deal of the adverse comment that his exuberant display had evoked.

It was the happiest Christmas Eve he had ever spent. To quote his own words, he had a rotten Christmas.

DOWN PENS

'Have you written to thank the Froplinsons for what they sent us?' asked Egbert.

'No,' said Janetta, with a note of tired defiance in her voice; 'I've written eleven letters today expressing surprise and gratitude for sundry unmerited gifts, but I haven't written to the Froplinsons.'

'Someone will have to write to them,' said Egbert.

'I don't dispute the necessity, but I don't think the someone should be me,' said Janetta.

'I wouldn't mind writing a letter of angry recrimination or heartless satire to some suitable recipient; in fact, I should rather enjoy it, but I've come to the end of my capacity for expressing servile amiability. Eleven letters today and nine yesterday, all couched in the same strain of ecstatic thankfulness: really, you can't expect me to sit down to another. There is such a thing as writing oneself out.'

'I've written nearly as many,' said Egbert, 'and I've had my usual business correspondence to get through, too. Besides, I don't know what it was that the Froplinsons sent us.'

'A William the Conqueror calendar,' said Janetta, 'with a quotation of one of his great thoughts for every day in the year.'

'Impossible,' said Egbert; 'he didn't have three hundred and sixty-five thoughts in the whole of his life, or, if he did, he kept them to himself. He was a man of action, not of introspection.'

'Well, it was William Wordsworth, then,' said Janetta; 'I know William came into it somewhere.'

'That sounds more probable,' said Egbert; 'well, let's collaborate on this letter of thanks and get it done. I'll dictate, and you can scribble it down. "Dear Mrs Froplinson — thank you and your husband so much for the very pretty calendar you sent us. It was very good of you to think of us."'

'You can't possibly say that,' said Janetta, laying down her pen.

'It's what I always do say, and what everyone says to me,' protested Egbert.

'We sent them something on the twenty-second,' said Janetta, 'so they simply HAD to think of us. There was no getting away from it.'

'What did we send them?' asked Egbert gloomily.

'Bridge-markers,' said Janetta, 'in a card-board case, with some inanity about "digging for fortune with a royal spade" emblazoned on the cover. The moment I saw it in the shop I said to myself "Froplinsons" and to the attendant "How much?" When he said

"Ninepence", I gave him their address, jabbed our card in, paid tenpence or elevenpence to cover the postage, and thanked heaven. With less sincerity and infinitely more trouble they eventually thanked me.'

'The Froplinsons don't play bridge,' said Egbert.

'One is not supposed to notice social deformities of that sort,' said Janetta; 'it wouldn't be polite. Besides, what trouble did they take to find out whether we read Wordsworth with gladness? For all they knew or cared we might be frantically embedded in the belief that all poetry begins and ends with John Masefield, and it might infuriate or depress us to have a daily sample of Wordsworthian products flung at us.'

'Well, let's get on with the letter of thanks,' said Egbert.

'Proceed,' said Janetta.

'"How clever of you to guess that Wordsworth is our favourite poet,"' dictated Egbert.

Again Janetta laid down her pen.

'Do you realise what that means?' she asked; 'a Wordsworth booklet next Christmas, and another calendar the Christmas after, with the same problem of having to write suitable letters of thankfulness. No, the best thing to do is to drop all further allusion to the calendar and switch off on to some other topic.'

'But what other topic?'

'Oh, something like this: "What do you think of the New Year Honours List? A friend of ours made such a clever remark when he read it." Then you can stick in any remark that comes into your head; it needn't be clever. The Froplinsons won't know whether it is or isn't.'

'We don't even know on which side they are in politics,' objected Egbert; 'and anyhow you can't suddenly dismiss the subject of the calendar. Surely there must be some intelligent remark that can be made about it.'

'Well, we can't think of one,' said Janetta wearily; 'the fact is, we've both written ourselves out. Heavens! I've just remembered Mrs Stephen Ludberry. I haven't thanked her for what she sent.'

'What did she send?'

'I forget; I think it was a calendar.'

There was a long silence, the forlorn silence of those who are bereft of hope and have almost ceased to care.

Presently Egbert started from his seat with an air of resolution. The light of battle was in his eyes.

'Let me come to the writing table,' he exclaimed.

'Gladly,' said Janetta. 'Are you going to write to Mrs Ludberry or the Froplinsons?'

'To neither,' said Egbert, drawing a stack of notepaper towards him; 'I'm going to write to the editor of every enlightened and influential newspaper in the Kingdom, I'm going to suggest that there should be a sort of epistolary Truce of God during the festivities of Christmas and New Year. From the twenty-fourth of December to the third or fourth of January it shall be considered an offence against good sense and good feeling to write or expect any letter or communication that does not deal with the necessary events of the moment. Answers to invitations, arrangements about trains, renewal of club subscriptions, and, of course, all the ordinary everyday affairs of business, sickness, engaging new cooks, and so forth, these will be dealt with in the usual manner as something inevitable, a legitimate part of our daily life. But all the devastating accretions of correspondence, incident to the festive season, these should be swept away to give the season a chance of being really festive, a time of untroubled, unpunctuated peace and good will.'

'But you would have to make some acknowledgment of presents received,' objected Janetta; 'otherwise people would never know whether they had arrived safely.'

'Of course, I have thought of that,' said Egbert; 'every present that was sent off would be accompanied by a ticket bearing the date of dispatch and the signature of the sender, and some conventional hieroglyphic to show that it was intended to be a Christmas or New Year gift; there would be a counterfoil with space for the recipient's name and the date of arrival, and all you would have to do would be to sign and date the counterfoil, add a conventional hieroglyphic indicating heartfelt thanks and gratified surprise, put the thing into an envelope and post it.'

'It sounds delightfully simple,' said Janetta wistfully, 'but people would consider it too cut-and-dried, too perfunctory.'

'It is not a bit more perfunctory than the present system,' said Egbert; 'I have only the same conventional language of gratitude at my disposal with which to thank dear old Colonel Chuttle for his perfectly delicious Stilton, which we shall devour to the last morsel, and the Froplinsons for their calendar, which we shall never look at. Colonel Chuttle knows that we are grateful for the Stilton, without having to be told so, and the Froplinsons know that we are bored with their calendar, whatever we may say to the contrary, just as we know that they are bored with the bridge-markers in spite of their written assurance that they thanked us for our charming little gift. What is more, the Colonel knows that even if we had taken a sudden aversion to Stilton or been forbidden it by the doctor, we should still have written a letter of hearty thanks around it. So you see the present system of acknowledgment is just as perfunctory and conventional as the counterfoil business would be, only ten times more tiresome and brain-racking.'

'Your plan would certainly bring the ideal of a Happy Christmas a step nearer realisation,' said Janetta.

'There are exceptions, of course,' said Egbert, 'people who really try to infuse a breath of reality into their letters of acknowledgment. Aunt Susan, for instance, who writes:

"Thank you very much for the ham; not such a good flavour as the one you sent last year, which itself was not a particularly good one. Hams are not what they used to be." It would be a pity to be deprived of her Christmas comments, but that loss would be swallowed up in the general gain.'

'Meanwhile,' said Janetta, 'what am I to say to the Froplinsons?'